My name is:

_____

Let's read my bedtime
story together.

some DAY

some NIGHT

Story by Jack Guinan

Illustrations by John Barilla

Visit www.amazon.com/author/jackguinan

ISBN-10: 1539456935

ISBN-13: 978-1539456933

Printed by CreateSpace.com. An Amazon.com Company

Available from Amazon.com and other retail outlets

Book design by Gladys Hunt www.greengigi.com

The sun
comes up,
high in the sky.
Then the moon
and stars
bid him
goodbye.

But what
would happen,
if this was not so,
and the sun decided
he wouldn't
go?

1

This is the tale
of one
such day,
when the sun
proclaimed,

"I'd like to stay!"

It all began
 like days before,
with a rooster's crow,
 a farmer's snore.

3

The flowers
awoke.
Their petals did yawn.
Happy birds
in the trees
sang out at dawn.

The sun was back,
for all to see.
On the horizon,
he rose
with
glee.

4

Throughout
the day,
the sun
shone bright.
The farmer in fields,
the birds
in flight.

Some clouds tiptoed in,
white against blue sky.
To join in
on the fun
they danced on by.

Both warm
and bright,
sun smiled down.
But then when he spoke,
smile,
turned frown.

6

"I am the sun,
who shines on you.

My rays keep you warm
the whole day through."

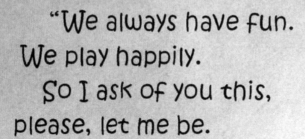

"We always have fun.
We play happily.
So I ask of you this,
please, let me be.

I love my friends
the stars and moon.
But it seems each day,
night comes
      too soon."

Everyone met,
high on the hill.
The farmer spoke first.
The birds
stood still.

"We all like you sun,
on this we agree.
But, you must
yield to night,
like shores
to sea."

9

The birds
chimed in,

"Yes sun, play fair.
You can't own the sky.
We all must share."

The
rooster
crowed
out,

"Cock-a-doodle-do!
If you don't
rise at dawn,
what shall
I do?"

Then came the wind,
swirling along.
He flew
by the sun.

What
could be
wrong?

Twisting and turning,
     he spun like a top.
          Until slowly the wind,
     came to a stop.

The sun was sad,
     hiding his face.

The wind
     then
          spoke up,
     calmly,
     with
          grace.

14

"Never think sun,
when you're
not here,
that we
don't love
you, that
you're
not
dear.

You're always with us.
Here, inside our hearts,
for we know
you'll be back,
when the day starts."

Sun then smiled,
ready for bed.
He thanked
all his friends,
winking
he
said,

"Sweet
dreams
await you.
They're your
special treat.
Get under your blankets.
Cover your feet."

17

"The stars and moon will soon appear. Stardust and moonbeams. Quickly. They're here!"

18

Then he was gone,
day turning night,
over the hillside,
beautiful sight.

Rainbow of colors,
red, yellow and blue.
A glorious sunset
sun's gift to you.

Everyone waved, saying goodbye, the moon and the stars, twinkling night sky.

20

So now
lay your head,
on pillow soft.
Dream under
night stars
in twilight's loft.

21

Our story has ended
at least for today.
And you,
like the sun
are loved every day.

Some day, some night.
Half dark, half light.
It's time now to sleep.
Sweet dreams.
Goodnight.

See more Jack Guinan books at

Made in the USA
Columbia, SC
20 May 2018